11/95 BT 14.73

BRAVE AS A TIGER

By Libuse Paleček
Illustrated by Josef Paleček

ENGLISH ADAPTATION BY ANDREW CLEMENTS

North-South Books / New York / London

When the little tiger was born, his mother named him Fang. It was a fierce name for such a little tiger, but his mother knew about the dangerous jungle. If you are a tiger and you live in the jungle, it's good to have a fierce name. And it's good to be strong. And it's especially good to be brave.

But the jungle didn't look dangerous to Fang. Flowers, trees, butterflies—it was beautiful.

One morning as Fang played outside his home, he heard a scary sound. He was terrified, so he lay down on the ground and curled up in a ball.

The sound came from other tigers—big, fearsome tigers.
"What's that whimpering little clump of fur there on the grass?"
one of them snorted.

"It's me, Fang. I—I'm a tiger too," he said. "See, I have stripes just like yours."

"You mean you HAD stripes!" And while the other tiger children watched and teased, the biggest, grumpiest tiger unbuttoned Fang's stripes and pulled them right off his furry coat! Then he growled, "And you won't get these stripes back until you deserve them!"

Fang felt sad without his stripes. He was sure his mother would be ashamed of him. So he said to himself, "I'm just going to run away. And I won't come back until I'm brave."

Fang left the jungle, and he came to an open field. There were clowns and acrobats and a ringmaster getting ready for the big circus. When the ringmaster saw him, he called out, "You there! Jump up onto this beam and do some tricks for me. I want you in my circus." But the man cracked his whip so loudly that it hurt Fang's ears, and then he lost his balance and tumbled off the beam. So Fang ran away.

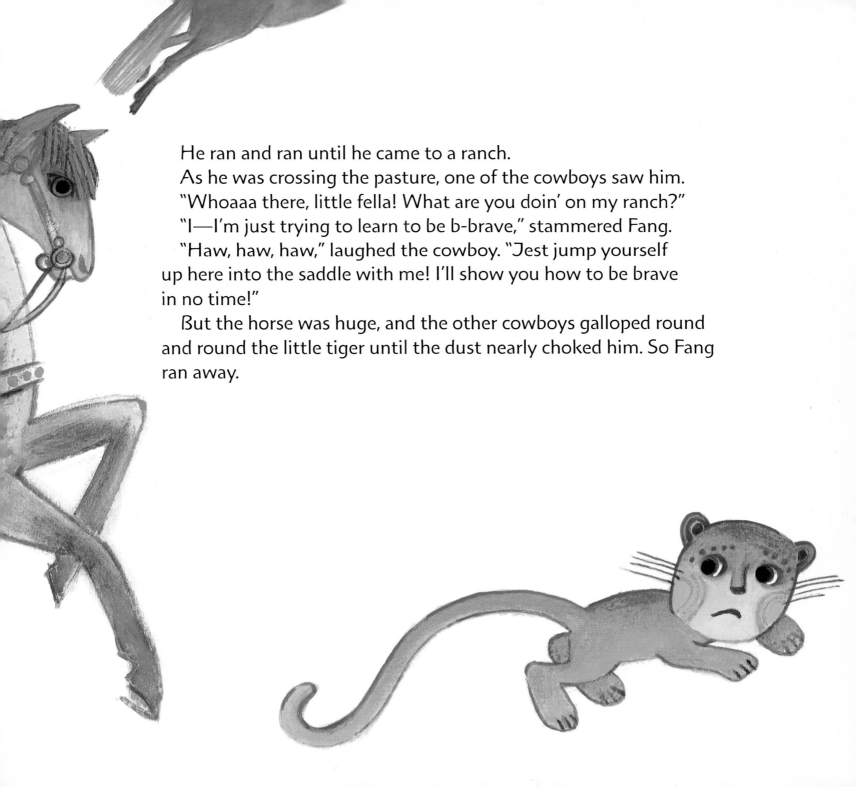

He ran and ran until he came to a ranch.

As he was crossing the pasture, one of the cowboys saw him.

"Whoaaa there, little fella! What are you doin' on my ranch?"

"I—I'm just trying to learn to be b-brave," stammered Fang.

"Haw, haw, haw," laughed the cowboy. "Jest jump yourself up here into the saddle with me! I'll show you how to be brave in no time!"

But the horse was huge, and the other cowboys galloped round and round the little tiger until the dust nearly choked him. So Fang ran away.

When night came, so did a storm. The wind howled and the trees moaned, and now Fang was more scared than ever. "I don't think I'll ever be brave," he said. And he ran back home as fast as he could.

"Mother . . . I'm home!" he called. But his mother didn't come to greet him. Fang went inside and found his mother in bed. She tried to get up, but she was too sick to move.

"You need help, Mother," said Fang. "I'm going to get the doctor." And before his mother could say a word, he was gone.

Fang ran through the jungle.
"FLASH!" went the lightning.
"BOOM!" went the thunder, and Fang stopped and shivered.
But he knew he had to help his mother, so he rushed on through the storm.

The path led to a deep ravine. The swollen river rushed and crashed to the rocks below, and the only way across was a narrow wooden bridge. Fang didn't even slow down. Straight across the bridge he went, on to get help.

The roots tripped him, the rain poured down, the lightning struck trees all around him, but Fang kept going.

And finally he saw a light—the doctor's house! Fang hammered on the door.

"Doctor, doctor! Please—my mother needs help!"

The doctor rushed to get his bag and his horse, and Fang jumped right up onto the saddle and sat in front. They galloped back towards his home. The bridge had washed away, but with a mighty leap the horse carried them safely across the river.

Soon the rain slowed down, and the moon even peeked out from behind a cloud.

They arrived safely, and the doctor rushed inside to care for Fang's mother. Fang stayed outside and fed the horse. The storm had blown away, and the stars were shining.

Then Fang heard that scary noise again, but this time he was not afraid.

The other tigers had come back.

"Are you the little tiger who rushed through the dark jungle alone to get the doctor?"

"Yes, I am," said Fang proudly.

"And are you the little tiger who went through the rain and the lightning and the thunder, who crossed the dangerous river twice—once on the back of a flying horse?"

"I'm the one," said the little tiger.

"Then we have something for you, Fang. Here are your stripes again. Among all the tigers in the jungle, no one deserves them more than you."

Mother soon felt better, so the doctor rode home. "Come along, my little tiger," said Mother. "You've had a very big day."

They went inside and climbed into bed, but Fang couldn't close his eyes. His mother patted his little striped arm and said, "Tonight you were brave in the very best way. I'm so happy for you."

And Fang smiled at his mother and whispered, "Me too."

Copyright © 1995 by Nord-Süd Verlag AG, Gossau Zürich, Switzerland
First published in Switzerland under the title NEIN ICH FÜRCHTE MICH NICHT
English translation copyright © 1995 by North-South Books Inc.

First published in the United States, Great Britain, Canada,
Australia, and New Zealand in 1995 by North-South Books,
an imprint of Nord-Süd Verlag AG, Gossau Zürich, Switzerland.

Distributed in the United States by North-South Books Inc., New York.

Library of Congress Cataloging-in-Publication Data is available.
A CIP catalogue record for this book is available from The British Library.
ISBN 1-55858-395-5 (TRADE BINDING)
1 3 5 7 9 TB 10 8 6 4 2
ISBN 1-55858-396-3 (LIBRARY BINDING)
1 3 5 7 9 LB 10 8 6 4 2
Printed in Belgium